CLAUDIA CARROLL

MIDSUMMER MIRACLE

Claudia Carroll is a top ten bestselling author in the UK and a number one bestselling author in Ireland, selling over 670,000 copies of her paperbacks alone. She was born in Dublin where she still lives. Her 2013 novel *Me and You* was shortlisted for the Bord Gais Popular Choice Irish Book Award. Her new novel, *Meet Me in Manhattan* will be published in March 2015 by Avon, HarperCollins.

NEW ISLAND

MIDSUMMER MIRACLE
First published 2015
by New Island
16 Priory Office Park
Stillorgan
Co Dublin

www.newisland.ie

PRINT ISBN: 978-1-84840-411-3

British Library Cataloguing Data. A CIP catalogue record
for this book is available from the British Library

Typeset by JVR Creative India
Cover design by New Island Books
Printed by SPRINT-print Ltd.

New Island received financial assistance from
The Arts Council (*An Comhairle Ealaíon*), Dublin, Ireland

10 9 8 7 6 5 4 3 2 1

Dear Reader,

On behalf of myself and the other contributing authors, I would like to welcome you to the eighth Open Door series. The books in this series are written and designed to introduce new and emergent readers to the writings of many bestselling authors who have sold millions of books worldwide. We hope that you enjoy the books and that reading becomes a lasting pleasure in your life.

Warmest wishes,

Patricia Scanlan

Patricia Scanlan
Series Editor

Please visit www.newisland.ie for information on all eight Open Door series.

Chapter One

'Now if you will all just follow me through the Red Drawing Room, it takes us on into the Long Gallery. This is the largest room in Radford Hall. In fact, it dates all the way back to 1779. It is a classic example of a building of that era at its most ornate. So if you will just look to your left . . .'

'Excuse me, Miss?' A kid with spiky, gelled hair interrupts, yelling at me from down the back. 'Can I ask you, something, Miss?' I pinpoint him as the class messer as soon as he starts yelling. Let's face it, there is always one. I brace myself.

'Great, go ahead!' I smile brightly. 'But please, call me Lizzie.'

'Well . . . it is a really big house and all, but there is no telly. I mean, you actually *live* here, don't you, Miss? On account of you being an actual Radford and everything.'

'I certainly do!' I answer proudly.

'So how do you manage without a telly, then? I mean, that is . . . *primitive!*'

'I bet she goes out fox hunting or something like that,' says a swotty looking boy. He wears a neatly ironed uniform and Harry Potter glasses. 'Don't you, Miss? People who live in posh houses like this are always mad into anything horsey and hunting to kill.'

'Not me, I'm afraid,' I assure him. 'And actually, there aren't any horses here at all, but . . .'

'Well then in that case, you must sit around, giving orders to butlers and house maids all day,' Swotty Kid insists. I hear more sniggers from the messers down the back. 'You know, like they do in *Downton Abbey* and all those old-lady TV shows my mum watches.'

'Sorry to disappoint you, but there are no full-time staff here, I'm afraid,' I smile back at him. 'In fact, I would say the last time anyone got paid to live and work here was long before your Granny was born. But just to let you know, I *do* have a TV. It is downstairs in the back kitchen.'

'And have you got Sky Plus on it?' The kid down the back with the spiky hair shouts up cheekily.

'Well, no!' I murmur. Mainly because I can't afford it. But I don't tell him that.

'*What?*'

'Yes, well . . . ah . . . just leaving the whole telly and Sky Plus issue aside for a minute, if you all would like to move down this way. I point to the Long Hall. I would really like to show you some of the Radford family drawings.'

They moan as I skip past the old paintings of all my dim, distant ancestors. You know the type. You have seen them in a dozen country houses. Plump women with very pale skin and no eyelashes. The husbands and sons, in their fancy pants and cloaks, glaring down on me. I imagine them saying, '*Is this what our home has been reduced to? You carry the great name, Radford. Just take a look at what you have done with it! Giving guided tours to a pack of bored school kids who could not care less!'*

'No offence, Miss,' says a very trendy looking girl with greasy black hair, 'but you look nothing like them. I mean, take this one,' she points to one of the paintings. 'She really is scary looking.'

I follow her finger and see that she is talking about my great-great grandmother Mary Barton, a daughter of the Earl of Curtis, who married into the Radfords. She brought lots of money to the family. It was likely the last time the family was rich.

'She's not Miss Universe, now is she?' jeered Miss Greasy Hair.

I have to admit, the kid is right. Poor old Mary looks tired and worn with having children. She looked as if she never got a good night's sleep in years.

'Yes, well, you have to remember this was painted when Mary was in her fifties,' I point out.

'I suppose in those days there was no such thing as hair products or even Mac bronzer,' says Greasy Hair helpfully. 'Because, you know, that would have made all the difference.'

'Excuse me, Lizzie!' says a blonde girl with braces and two pink slides in her hair. 'There is a load of pots down the back of that funny looking sofa! And they are full of dirty water! It looks a bit like cat wee. Look!'

More giggles as they all dive to have a look for themselves. I am suddenly aware of thirty pairs of eyes all turning back to me. The class stares at me, just waiting to hear what is going on behind the sofa.

I turn bright red, right up to the roots of my hair. 'Well you know, the roof here at Radford Hall is well over two hundred years old, so there is the odd little patch of it that may be just a tiny bit leaky,' I tell them. I am embarrassed and mad with myself for not thinking to empty the rain water out of the pots earlier.

'The wallpaper is peeling off in places too. Look!' says Pink Slide Girl. I just know that this girl will be a pest to estate agents later in life.

'What is that funny smell in here?' asks her tall, thin friend who is clamped to her side. She looks as if the tour is some kind of torture for her. I know she would rather be trawling through the rails at Topshop.

'Oh, that!' I manage a weak smile, trying my best to laugh it off. 'That is absolutely nothing. Just, you know, old houses have their own distinct, special smell. This house is no different. Don't worry, you will get used to it in time!'

'It is damp, that is what it is,' says Pink Slide Girl, arms folded. 'My dad works in construction and he says damp is a health hazard. Are you not at all worried, Lizzie?'

Not if you saw the size of my bank overdraft, love, I think, forcing my jaw into a grin and trying not to grit my teeth.

'Anyway, leaving the smell of damp aside for the moment,' I manage to say, 'if we can just get back to the family paintings.'

'Bloody freezing in here too,' yawns a porky looking kid, who has flopped down into an armchair, like a tenant who has just moved in.

'It sure is!' says a voice from the back of the room. 'And I wouldn't mind, but it is the middle of June! It is roasting outside, but you would swear it was January in here!'

'Is there even a Starbucks or something, where we can all go and get lunch?' Porky Kid demands. 'And, like, maybe warm up a bit?'

'The nearest coffee shop is in the town, I'm afraid. Now I would like to tell you a bit about this painting here. There's a really interesting story behind it. You see . . .'

'You know something? I think it's actually warmer outside than it is in here,' Pink Slide Girl says cheekily, to more giggles from the rest of her classmates, which of course they know right well they can get away with.

Their teacher was last seen outside having a sneaky fag behind the school bus.

'In fact, if you ask me, this house is unfit for human living,' Pink Slide Girl goes on. 'I told my dad we were coming here on a school trip today and he said Radford Hall should have been destroyed years ago.'

I swear to God, the child can't be more than about thirteen and I want to strangle her with the glittery bit off her ponytail.

And to make it worse, the little madam is only telling the truth. Radford Hall looks stunning on the outside. The sad fact is, the minute you step inside, you can see the decay it has fallen into. The even sadder fact is, I am moving Heaven and earth to do everything I can to keep the old place going. The small bit of money I make from school tours is not enough to keep the house in good condition. Pink Slide Girl has a point. You would really want to be insane to live here.

'Miss Lizzie, do you really live here all on your own?' asks a pale, red-haired girl who looks very worried.

'That's right,' I smile back at her.

'You mean you have no husband or brothers and sisters to help you out?'

'No, and I am an only child,' I tell her. 'So it is up to me to keep things going here, you see.'

'And where are your parents then?'

Funny, but ever since I moved here just over six months ago, I have become used to answering these questions.

'Both my parents passed away when I was just a small child, I'm afraid,' I say.

'My dad told me about that,' says Pink Slide Girl, nodding her head. 'Car crash, wasn't it?'

'That's right.' I nod back,

'Shush,' her very thin pal beside her hisses, shooting her an angry look and digging her in the ribs. 'We were told not to even mention that.'

An uneasy silence falls as the kids all look from one to the other. I can see that they are sorry for me, and are mortified at the same time.

'That is awful, Miss.'

'Sorry to hear it, Miss.'

I give a tiny smile and hope that we can leave the more painful parts of my family history at that. After all, it happened well over twenty years ago.

'So you see, I inherited this house from my Uncle Edward, who passed away just a few months ago,' I tell them, hoping we can all move on, but no such luck.

'And did he have it in for you or what?' comes a muffled voice from the back. 'He must have done, to land this kip on you!'

I try not to let the insult upset me.

'But does that mean that you are totally alone here?' Pale Red Head Girl asks. 'Do you not have a boyfriend either?'

'I am afraid not, no.' I wish they would all clear off.

'That is so sad, Miss,' she says, shaking her head, looking at me with big sad eyes. 'To be all alone in the world.'

'Well, it is not *that* sad really. Come on, there is nothing wrong with being single and living by yourself!'

'Of course there is, Miss! It is okay when you are young, but you are like, really old now,' she insists. 'If you were ever going to get married, you would have done it by now.'

'Well I am not really old, am I? I'm only twenty-nine' I tell her, a bit annoyed.

'Oh, Miss, that is even worse! *Miles* older than I would have given you! Twenty-nine and living all alone in a place like this is just so . . . *sad*. You poor thing. I feel really sorry for you.'

'But I am perfectly happy living alone, I promise you!'

'You know what? You should totally try internet dating,' says a really cool, model type girl. She is wearing fluffy cream Ugg boots. I dislike her purely because I could never afford them.

'My sister is older too, though she is not nearly as old as you, Miss, but anyway, that is where she met her last three boyfriends. There is a site called It's Just Lunch and you just meet in a café and you just take it from there. My sister says, once you learn how to avoid the saddos, whackos and weirdos, you can find some really lovely guys online. And even if you do not fancy the one you do meet, it is just an hour out of your day. The key thing to remember Miss is that it's just lunch.' She tosses her glossy, silky hair over her shoulders, like someone who has done it all.

'True,' I say calmly, pretending to be cool about it. 'Well I am not certain how we managed to get diverted from our house tour to talking about my love life and online dating, but I really do want you all to take a look at this painting, right here.' I try to take control of the situation.

'Or you know, if dating websites do not do it for you, Miss,' Ugg Boot Girl walks over to me, with all the confidence of those who are born beautiful, 'then you could always just stick to Facebook, you know. My auntie is this older person, like you. She says Facebook is a total pick-up joint these days. Better than any nightclub or bar, she thinks. You can meet guys from the comfort of home, with awful unwashed hair and no make-up. It might just suit you, Miss.'

'Yes well, thanks *so* much for that,' I say, aware that the entire class seem to be far more interested in my love life than they ever were in the tour. In fact, it is the first time all morning that you could hear a pin drop. 'But, you know, we really do need to get back to the tour now.'

'Miss, I have another question for you,' says the pale, worried-looking girl who bloody well started all this.

'About Radford Hall, I hope!'

'Well, sort of. Are you not a bit afraid here, all by yourself, Miss? I would be petrified. A single woman, all on her own in a place this size? It must be terrifying! And the nearest town is miles away. If a murderer *did* break in, you would not stand a chance. It would take ages for the police to even get here. By then, he would probably have chopped you up and buried you under the patio.'

'God knows why anyone would bother breaking into a freezing kip like this,' I can clearly overhear Pink Slide Girl muttering to her pal. 'Sure there isn't even anything worth stealing.'

'And I bet that you have got ghosts here too,' Worried Girl goes on, looking at me kindly. 'Old ruins like this always have unhappy spirits floating around. It is a miracle you manage to get any sleep here at all.'

I smile and try to rise above the 'old ruin' comment. I resist the urge to say that the only evil spirit haunting me these days is my bank manager. I am aware by now that the entire class is looking at me and I can almost see what they are all thinking. They have all gone and formed this view that I lead this lonely single life, in a house I cannot afford to heat, that I am living on the set of a horror film, scared that an axe-murderer will come and get me.

Most of that is rubbish. After all, it is not like I have not had the odd romance since I moved here all those months ago. Okay, so maybe it was more flirtation in my mind, but still. I do actually meet guys. Well, to be more correct, I did actually meet one guy, an unmarried one too, even if he did happen to be spoken for.

My mind wanders, just thinking about him, but then I am instantly pulled back to the class. They all stand silently, staring up at me. They are shuffling and looking bored stiff. Some send worried glances my way.

It is like the entire class is now taking in the awful state of Radford Hall. I know they are thinking that, posh house or no posh house, they would far rather go home to the warmth and comfort of their own homes.

Right now I wish they would!

Chapter Two

'So how much did you make today on that tour then, love? Anything worth telling me about?'

'Trust me, you do not want to know,' I say, trying to laugh it off and cover up just how worried I am under my bright smile.

I am sitting downstairs in the old kitchen at Radford Hall. Opposite me, mug of tea in her hand, is lovely Mrs Butterly. She was my Uncle Edward's housekeeper. I cannot afford to pay her, but she still comes up to the Hall to visit me every so often. She always brings a plate of ham sandwiches or a pot of her chicken stew.

Bless her kind heart. Every so often I will even catch her waving a duster round the place to help me out a bit. But then Mrs Butterly looked after Uncle Edward for so long, I think she finds cleaning here a hard habit to break. Plus, I know right well that she is worried about me being here all by myself. Mrs Butterly feels I am in need of company.

'Total profit from this afternoon's tour is a staggering one hundred and five euro. Oh God, that is barely enough to cover this month's electricity bill.'

I am staring down at the spreadsheet in front of me. My two feet are pressed up against the cooker. It is the only way to warm up around here. Even during the summer.

'Ah, come on now, love,' says Mrs Butterly, doing her best to sound happy and upbeat. She tops up our mugs of tea and passes me another ham sandwich, which I gratefully bite into. 'Money is coming in and after all, that is the main thing.'

It is unsaid between us, but the view is there all the same. There is not enough money to keep the place surviving. Not nearly enough to cover the bills. Short of me finding oil in the ground, my dream of restoring the Hall back to its former glory is useless.

As ever, Mrs Butterly can read my mind.

'Do you know something, love?' she says, blue eyes looking sharply at me now. 'I remember your Dad, God be good to him, when he was still in short trousers, coming round here to see your Uncle Edward. And I know that he would be dead proud of you and of what you are trying to do here. When he met your Mum, she fell in love with the Hall too. They even had their wedding here. It was quite the posh occasion. They really loved the old place, just like you do, you know. And remember, just because they are not here in person, does not mean they are not looking after you from the other side. Trust me on that, love.'

'Thanks,' I say, my eyes growing wet with tears. But then I love whenever Mrs Butterly tells me stories of my Dad as a kid. And tales about my Mum and him, when they were first married. Somehow, it fills in the blurry picture I have of them both. I was very young when I lost them. I grew up with my Auntie in London. She was Mum's sister. She would chat away about Mum, but she barely knew Dad at all.

'So just do not give up,' Mrs Butterly adds. 'Do not ever give up.'

I am just about to lean over and pat her hand warmly, when we are suddenly interrupted by the sound of tires on the gravel outside, which at this time of the evening is very unusual.

'Are you expecting someone?' Mrs Butterly asks, eyes darting over to the window.

'Me? Expecting a gentleman caller round here? That is a laugh! And it is too late in the evening for it to be someone else asking about a tour.'

In a moment, we are both up on our feet and heading for the window for a peek, Mrs Butterly waddling as fast as she can in front of me. She pulls the curtains shut as she realizes who it is.

'I do not believe it! It is them! Again!'

'Oh God, no! Please tell me you are joking!'

'For the love of God, would you just shut up and HIDE!' hisses Mrs Butterly. She has her back to the wall now, like some kind of hostage in a drama. 'Quick, before they see you!'

I move the curtain on the window beside me and take a quick look outside.

There was a black jeep parked outside with a 2008 Dublin registration plate.

Hell! It only meant one thing. I instantly knew why my unwanted visitors had landed in on top of me this evening. More importantly, I knew exactly what it was they had come to say.

It was Paddy and Jada just dropping in for one of their regular check-ups on me, disguised as a friendly chat. It is happening once a month at this stage. In fact, I could almost set my watch by the pair of them.

'Ah, to hell with this anyway,' says Mrs Butterly. 'I could not face that pair of bloodsuckers tonight, not for the life of me. No offence, Lizzie, I know you are related to them and everything, but I am going to make a run for it out the back door before they see me.'

'But how will you get home?' I protest.

'It is fine. I have my bike with me. I will get away without having to face them, do not worry, Lizzie love. And if you've any sense, you should come with me!'

But it is too late now. It is early Friday evening. They know this is a good time to catch me at home. They know I will be getting ready to go out. I always go to the village for my usual Friday night supper with my pal, Hilary. When it comes to these particular visitors, I have found that it is far easier just to take a deep breath, keep cool and get it over with.

I hug Mrs Butterly goodbye and thank her warmly. She hurries out the back door. I run across the heavy flagstones on the kitchen, up a flight of stairs and over the cold stone of the long corridor. I reach the main entrance hall. Then, pushing open the heavy oak door, I step out into the warm evening sunlight to face the firing squad.

'Lizzie!' says Paddy, wrapping me in a bear hug. 'I am so glad that we caught you! We were just passing and we thought we would drop in.'

Just passing, yeah right, I think. I plaster on a fake grin. Jada strides across the gravel and lightly air-kisses me.

'Hi, Lizzie,' she miles. 'It is so lovely to see you! Any chance of a coffee? It has been ages and we would love to have a good catch-up with you.'

'Ah . . . great to see you too, and I am so sorry about this, but I am actually off to meet a pal,' I tell them, delighted to have a solid excuse to get out of there.

'Oh, I am sure your pal will not mind if you are a bit delayed,' Paddy says bossily, not making eye contact with me. Instead, he is staring at the Hall behind me. I know he is preparing for the day when he can let lots of estate agents loose on the place.

I should explain. Paddy Radford is not only my cousin, but is my nearest living relative. Jada is his wife. She is all shiny hair, skinny jeans and perfect teeth. You know the type. Anyway, they live up in Dublin. Their kids are in posh private schools. The pair of them were the richest people I knew, until the recession hit. Paddy's property management company collapsed, which, according to them, was everyone's fault, except his.

But instead of just cutting back, like the rest of us have had to, their solution is to cling tightly to their five-star lifestyle. They had to sell off any excess property they had, including their holiday apartment in Marbella and the pony they'd bought for their eldest daughter.

Now that they have run out of family silver to sell, they are looking with greedy eyes at Radford Hall. Long story, but the bottom line is, if it were ever to be sold, Paddy is a Radford and has a right to part of the sale. It is all there, laid out clearly in Uncle Edward's will. So Paddy feels he has a right to tell me what to do with the place, no matter how I feel.

So with a sick feeling in my stomach, I know exactly why they are here, and what it is they want to say to me. It is the same thing they have been saying for the last year, ever since I first came to the Hall.

'So where are you meeting your pal?' Paddy asks.

'At the Radford Arms. I was just about to stroll down there now, so if you will excuse me,' I say firmly.

'Hop in so, we will drive you,' Paddy says, smiling sweetly.

'Not at all! It is a lovely evening, I will walk!'

'Would not hear of it. Sure, we are driving through Avoca anyway. And we can have a nice little chat in the car.'

Damn it. No way of avoiding what is coming. I climb up into the back seat and we race back down the driveway. They lock the doors, so I feel trapped, as if I am being held captive.

To set the scene, Radford Hall is in Wicklow. It is pretty isolated and set in twenty acres of land. It was, at one time, some of the most beautiful rolling land in the county. Now it is one big jungle.

The nearest town is Avoca in Wicklow. It looks perfect and that is where I am headed. So I am stuck with this pair for the next ten minutes, in a locked car and no way out.

'You are looking so tired, Lizzie,' Jada says, turning back to me from the passenger seat, pretending to be concerned. 'Even more so than the last time we called to see you. Look at you! You are absolutely exhausted. Isn't she, Paddy?'

'It is because she is wearing herself out trying to keep that house in shape,' he says, shaking his head and focusing on the road ahead. Every now and then, I catch him taking sneaky looks back me in the mirror. I know he is trying to see just how far he can push me

'Paddy is absolutely right, you know,' says Jada. I notice her big engagement ring is gone – things must be that bad. 'And at the end of the day, is it really worth all the hassle?'

'As a matter of fact, everything is going fine at the Hall,' I lie. 'It is better than fine, in fact, it is wonderful! I had a school tour in today, very successful. And well-paid too.'

'Yes, but you have to admit, it is still a huge struggle for you,' Paddy says, shaking his head sadly. 'Breaks my heart to see you trying to make the place make money, when we all know the days of big houses are long over.'

'I mean, look at the state of it!' says Jada. 'It needs millions spent on it, just to make it suitable for living in.'

'No one has that kind of money these days.'

'But I will tell you who does have that kind of money.' Jada says. 'Rich Irish people coming back to Ireland from abroad. You know, guys who have made their money. Now they are looking for a slice of classic county life in a stately home. Let's face it, it is a buyer's market right now.'

'Good point Jada,' Paddy smirks at his wife. 'And you know, these people actually have the money to spend on places like Radford Hall. They would be well able to improve it and restore it, back to what it should be.'

For God's sake! I think, feeling like steam is starting to pour out of my ears, as if I were in a cartoon. Did the pair of them rehearse this on the way down? I would not put it past them. They are starting to sound a bit like Tweedle Dum and Tweedle Dee from *Alice in Wonderland*. I have been listening to the very same conversation for months now.

'Just think about selling, Lizzie,' says Paddy. 'That is all I am saying. And you know, I have a lot of contacts in the property world. I would be glad to make all the arrangements for you. You would not have to do a thing. You could pay off your loan and all the taxes that came with getting this house.'

'And still have a fortune left over to buy a lovely little flat in town.

Somewhere warm and cozy and easy to keep,' Jada chimes in.

'A flat where you would not be so alone, and then we would not have to worry about you struggling here all on your own . . .'

'Worry about me?' I want to scream at them. My eyes are blazing now from the sheer annoyance of having to listen to this load of crap. They are worried about me? They were so worried, that over the whole of last Christmas, I never even got a phone call from them. Their Christmas gift was a fridge magnet with an estate agent's logo stuck on the back of it, just in case I would miss the hint.

Finally, we arrive at the outskirts of Avoca. Within two seconds I am out of the car door and saying goodbye to them through the window.

'Well thanks so much for the lift,' I tell them crisply, failing to keep the anger out of my voice. 'But about that other matter, I would not hold my breath if I were you.'

'Do not be stubborn, Lizzie,' says Paddy. 'You know as well as we do that you are fighting a losing battle.'

'It is not that simple,' I tell him honestly. 'You know Radford Hall has been in our family for over two hundred years. I would go to my grave before I saw it being sold. Not now, not on my watch.'

'Lizzie, you have got to stop holding onto this romantic ideal about the place and try to see some sense. There is a massive loan on the place. If things keep going the way they are, how are you ever going to meet your repayments?' Paddy made his parting shot.

The honest answer to this question is, I do not know. Instead, I stride on in the direction of the Radford Arms. Rage fuels me onwards, but just walking along the country street calms me down. The main street is covered in decorations and jammed packed with people on their way to the Midsummer Fair. There were lots of hyper kids full of chocolate and ice cream their parents looking forward to the fun ahead. In spite of my rage, my spirits slowly begin to lift.

I do not care what Paddy Radford thinks and that is all there is to it. I am *not* insane to try to take on such a massive project that may fail. And Mum and Dad would be proud of what I am trying to do. My eyes fall on a giant poster outside one of the shops that says 'Happy Midsummer to one and all!'

Then, out of nowhere, something my mother always used to say comes back to me.

'Magic happens at Midsummer.' I can still hear her saying it to me when I was little. 'Always remember that, Lizzie love, and always trust it. If anything ever happens to me, I will be sure to send you a Midsummer miracle. All you need to do is trust it. Magic can and will happen.'

And today is that day. It is June the twenty-first.

Mum, Dad? I find myself silently praying to them both. If you are looking down on me now, if you can see me at all . . . can you find me my Midsummer miracle?

God knows, I have never needed one more.

Chapter Three

'Wow the creeps you are related to!' Hilary almost splutters into her bowl of chicken pasta when I tell her about my unwanted visitors.

'I know,' I nod, taking another calming sip of white wine, a lovely Friday night treat Hilary treated us both to.

'Dollar signs lit up in Paddy Radford's little greedy eyes, I suppose?'

'Like you would not believe.'

'And the wife probably had her measuring tape out all ready to get the place on the market first thing in the morning,' Hilary jeered.

'Well not quite, but not too far off.' I dip my garlic bread into some creamy sauce.

'Never trust a man with his eyes too close together,' my friend warns. 'And you have to admit, Paddy definitely has a look of a rat about him'

'I know, love, I know,' I tell her soothingly, topping up her glass of wine. She gratefully knocks it back.

'You see, this is what makes me so angry!' she says, working herself up into a state of anger. 'Paddy and Jada see a single woman on her own in a house that size. They not only assume that you are not managing, but they also assume that you will jump at the chance to just walk away from something that you have worked so hard for. I mean, you are doing everything possible to keep the place afloat!'

I look across the table at her fondly. This is why everyone should have a Hilary in their lives, I think. There are no grey areas with her, she just sees everything in black and white. On nights like this, you have got to love her attitude.

The Radford Arms is packed tonight. The Midsummer Fair is in full swing. The pair of us have managed to find a cosy table right at the back. The place is a very popular pub and restaurant. Hilary has been waitressing in it for a long time, and we have been friends from the start.

Word went out the among the locals that old Mr Edward Radford's niece was taking over the Hall after he suddenly passed away.

So there I was, months ago, after moving in, rattling around this massive estate. I could vaguely remember visiting with my parents as a small child. There had been a knocking on the hall door. When I unlocked it, there was this super-beautiful creature, six feet tall and stick-thin, with bobbed jet-black hair. She wore the thickest black eyeliner I have ever seen. She was dressed all in black. She held two things in her hands: welcome basket of muffins, that she had baked herself, and a bottle of champagne

'Welcome to the country,' she grinned at me. 'I'm Hilary O'Reilly. I could not handle the idea of you here all by yourself on your first night. So what do you say we get this party started?'

And that was it, mates from that day to this.

'And I would not mind,' Hilary goes on, tearing off a giant lump of garlic bread and soaking up the rest of her sauce with it, 'but it is not like you are hanging around up there, lying on a sofa like Lady Mary from bloody *Downton Abbey*. Look at you, you are working your ass off!'

'I have a massive loan to pay back and my guided tours are not earning what I need,' I moan.

Hilary, bless her, is too understanding to go into it any further.

'And you know something else?' I say, pushing my empty plate away and falling back into the seat. 'I think that is what really gets me more than anything, you know? Everyone around me seems to think that I am crazy to even try to keep a place the size of Radford Hall. But they do not get it! No one seems to understand that I actually do love it there. I really adore the old place. And yes, I know it is run- down and I know it has seen better days, but I love living there. I love country life. What is more, I know that if Mum and Dad were still around, they would do exactly the same thing. So in a way, I am doing it in their name, not just my own. I just know it is what they would have wanted.'

There is a short pause while Hilary looks worriedly at me. Sometimes even talking about my parents can bring me to tears. I still miss them both so much, every day.

But that is the funny thing about grief. Time goes by, until one day you think that you are fine. Then just something simple like coming across a childhood photo of your Dad, and you are upset for the rest of the day. But right now I do a quick check of my feelings and realise that it is actually okay. I am able to talk about them both, out loud.

Maybe it is because it is Midsummer. As Mum always said, a time when miracles can, and do, happen.

'I understand,' Hilary says gently. 'And if no one else gets it, then I promise you, at least I do.'

I smile gratefully back at her. 'You are such a good pal,' I say.

'So come on now, love,' Hilary says, shoving her empty plate away. 'After all, it is Friday night. There is a party in full swing outside. For once, I am not working tonight. What do you say we have a few drinks, kick our shoes off and just for tonight forget all our troubles?'

'Sounds like a plan to me!'

'Oh . . . and by the way, Andy is on his way up from Dublin,' she throws in casually. But then I know Hilary well enough by now to understand what she is really saying.

'Oh, really?' I answer, trying my best to sound all cool. 'And is he bringing Eva with him?' That is his girlfriend. You don't want to know. Trust me.

'Well no, as it happens. He said he had loads to tell me. By the sounds of it, they have finally broken up. No surprise there. I always knew that Eva was trouble. God knows, I have certainly told Andy enough times.'

My friend looks at me and I find myself blushing. To explain, Andy is Hilary's older brother. And he is the crush I mentioned during the grilling I got about my love life from the school kids this morning. Hilary is in a fairly long-term relationship. She is on a mission to get me matched up with someone, and as soon as possible.

She is dating a Polish guy called Tomas. She met him in our local Tesco store about a year ago. Hilary left without paying the twenty-two cents for a plastic bag at the self-service check out. It was not done on purpose. Tomas chased her down the street. Her side of the story is that she did a great job arguing with him. She claimed it was an honest mistake and if he did not think so, then he could get lost. Tomas just burst out laughing at her and asked for her phone number instead.

Tomas's side of the story was that Hilary burst into tears. She said this was a big mistake on his part. She declared that she was going to ring a local politician and a Garda that she knew from drinking in the Radford Arms. *And* she was going on the Joe Duffy show to tell the nation about the abuse she had experienced.

So Tomas got her to relax and decided to let her away with the twenty-two cents. Hilary was so grateful she asked if she could repay him by taking him out for a drink sometime. Anyway, whatever version you decide to go along with, the important thing was that somehow, they ended up together.

So now of course she is on a mission to get me matched up. As long as he does not end up sailing into my life from the internet dating sites. Believe me, I have had my share of disasters there. Hilary was the one who was there to pick up the pieces.

In my defence, though, I am always telling her that single men around my own age are as rare as hen's teeth round here. Like it or not, internet dating is as important to our generation as the dancehall was to our grannies back in the sixties.

'So,' she says, looking at sternly. 'Are you still messing around on those internet dating sites these days?'

'Now and again,' I tell her.

'They are such a waste of your time, and energy! Will you ever forget that prat you met from Belfast?' She is laughing now, draining the last of her wine.

I wish Hilary had not brought up that event. That was last Christmas. I was happily messaging a dish called Dan, a teacher from the North. I instantly thought he was someone caring, sensitive and honest. Ha! Read on!

Anyway, online messages turned to phone calls. When the time came for Dan and I to have that important first meeting, I instantly got suspicious. He claimed that he was not free at weekends or evenings, just weekdays only. And by weekdays, I mean nine to five. During the day! Evenings were out. The final giveaway was when

Hilary and I scanned his profile photo, the one where he looked really handsome in a morning suit. It was taken when he was best man at his brother's wedding, Dan had told me shamelessly.

It was Hilary. 'Tall Dan lies,' as she pointed out. And sure enough, if you looked at the photo closely, you could just about make out his bride's arm. Dan had cut her out of the picture.

I was keen to change the subject. I leaned back against my chair, and yawned.

'Now I know you have too much time to yourself up at the Hall these days,' Hilary says, with a big lump of pasta wobbling at the end of her fork, 'Trust me. Just try spending a wee bit more time with *real* people and your prince will come along soon enough. Maybe a lot sooner than you think.'

'Well do not hold your breath!' I laugh back at her.

'So come on then. The party is just getting going outside. How about we wander out and take a look?'

'Sounds like a plan to me,' I grin.

Chapter Four

We gather up our bags and make our way towards the door. We aim to get to the beer garden when Dave Sullivan, the owner, and Hilary's boss, calls us back.

'Hang on a minute, ladies, are you not both forgetting something?'

She and I both turn and look at him blankly.

'Ah, Dave, come on! It is my night off tonight!' Hilary starts protesting. 'I have been working really hard all week!'

'Nothing to do with work, you dope,' Dave grins. He turns on the TV. 'Well, it is Friday night, yeah?' he says, surprised that we have somehow overlooked this.

'And what about it?' Hilary demands.

'Well, Friday night Euromillions draw is coming on any minute now. Just hang on a second until we check our numbers.'

Oh God, here we go. Yet again. We have got a village group going, you see. It been had been going for years before I moved here. In all that time, it has never even returned a single lousy scratch card. Hilary is in it. So is Dave and half the staff at the Radford Arms. I was dragged into it, thanks to Hilary, when I first came here.

'Ah forget it, Dave!' Hilary laughs, steering me away from the TV and out into the warm sunshine outside.

And yet something stops me in my tracks. I know it is hopeless. I know you have about as much chance of winning as being struck by a bolt of lightning. I know it is a complete waste of time. I also know what Warren Buffet famously said that state lotteries are 'nothing but a tax on fools.'

But my mother's words keep coming back to me.

If anything ever happens to me, I will be sure to send you a Midsummer miracle.

'Just hang on a second,' I tell Hilary. I stare up towards the telly. 'Come on, it will only take a second.'

The wheel begins to spin and the first number is called.

'Three!'

'Yes, that is one of mine,' says Dave. 'Date of my wedding anniversary. I would be murdered if I ever forgot that one!'

A few bursts of laughter and then we are all back to looking at the screen overhead. An attractive, middle-aged guy with a booming voice is presenting it tonight. Some wag at the back of the pub pipes up, 'Lads, if I ever won a few quid on the Lotto, I will tell you what I would do. I would get some hair plugs put in your man! Isn't he the right silver fox, all the same?'

'Shut up!' a few other voices hiss as we watch the big screen.

The second number is . . . seventeen.

'We have that too!' yells Tina, another barmaid who has abandoned clearing the tables. She is glued to the telly like the rest of us. 'Date of my daughter's birthday. Seventeen is always lucky for me, you know!'

More shushing and 'keep it down, will you, love?' as Marty Whelan keeps reading out the results.

Third and fourth numbers are 'twenty-four and twenty-six!' announces Marty, with a little sideways wink towards the TV camera.

'I do not believe this! Twenty-four is mine!' screeches Hilary, 'it is the date of my birthday!'

'Sweet Baby Jesus and the orphans,' says Tom Butterly, Mrs Butterly's husband. He is a Saturday night regular in here. He even has his own bar stool. 'Lads, we've got twenty-six too!' he says hammering a big fist gleefully on the bar. 'That is my one, it is the number of my house!'

'Only way you can remember your way home, after you have had a few too many pints in here, Tom, isn't that right?' Tina teases him, to yet more calls for quiet up the front.

The whole pub is gone very silent now. I swear you can almost feel people suddenly daring to dream. After all, we have never come this far before. Not once. Never.

'Just two more . . . that is all we need,' says Dave quietly from behind the bar. For a second, my heart goes out to him. His business has been suffering a lot since the economic downturn. Things are not easy in the bar trade generally. Like me, in fact, like most of us, I know he's in debt up to his eyeballs. If there ever was anyone who deserved a bit of luck to go their way, it was Dave.

'Fifth number is,' says Marty, the sound on the telly now turned up to almost deafening levels now, 'number twelve!'

And now there is total silence as we all look glance around at each other. All hoping and praying that someone in our syndicate will claim it. After a heart-stopping pause, Mrs Kelly, an elderly pensioner who lives in sheltered housing nearby, speaks up.

'What did she say? Was it twelve? I could not hear the telly properly. My hearing aid needs new batteries.'

'Yes, twelve!' The rest of us repeat back at her. The tension is practically pinging off the four walls by now.

'Oh well, wait till I see what number I did this week. Sorry, everyone, my memory is not what it used to be.'

There are nervy looks on everyone's faces and I swear, Hilary is now gripping my hand and I think she is in danger of cutting off my circulation.

'I know I wrote it down here somewhere,' says poor old Mrs Kelly, spilling the contents of her handbag out onto the table. She rummages like a mad woman. 'I am almost certain I wrote it down on the back of a bus ticket.'

'My nerves,' mutters Dave beside me. He is as white as a ghost and sweating buckets. There is another awful silence worthy of a Samuel Becket play. Then, thank you, God, Mrs Kelly finally pipes up. 'Here we are! I knew I went to the bother of writing it down somewhere!' she says, waving a bus ticket joyfully.

'For God's sake, what number did you have?' asks Tom from the bar.

'Oh, sorry,' she says, sounding frail and a bit confused now. 'I must have left my reading glasses at home. I cannot see what this says. Can someone read it out for me?'

I actually think I might pass out with the tension as Hilary springs to the old lady's side. She takes the bus ticket and reads it. Then slowly, to total silence from the whole bar, she looks back up again. She is white-faced and more shocked than I have ever seen her.

'It's twelve,' is all she says softly. 'It's actually twelve.'

'Oh yes, yes, yes, now I remember,' smiles Mrs Kelly, thrilled with herself.

'Of course, that is my number. Date of my late husband's anniversary. How could I have forgotten?'

'So then . . . that means . . .' Hilary says, turning to look over at me.

'It means we just need one more,' I answer, stunned. My vision is starting to blur a bit with all the tension.

'And what is the jackpot tonight?' someone asks.

'It was a rollover from last week. So . . . so . . . it is around forty-five million.'

I find myself gasping. Forty-five million, split ten ways among our little syndicate. A fortune. An absolute *fortune*.

I could pay off my loans and renovate the Hall. Restore it to what it could be. A proper family home again.

I could, for once in my whole life, really live the dream. We *all* could.

I look at Hilary who is back by my side. She is holding my hand so tightly now, I can barely feel it. Hilary could do what she has always wanted to do, too. Set up her own business. Open her very own restaurant. And still have plenty of change to spare!

But no, we could not be that lucky. Could we? Sure everyone knows you are more likely to be run over by a space shuttle than for a miracle like this to happen. Don't they? True, it would be a rotten twist of fate to have come this close and to lose out now. But that is life, isn't it?

Right then Mum's words come back to me. 'Miracles happen at Midsummer.'

'Come on,' says Dave. 'Come on. Just one more.'

'What is our last number anyway?' says Tara Quinn, a mother of four kids. They are all under the age of seven. She needs cash almost as badly as I do myself.

'It is mine,' I tell the room in a tiny voice. 'Number nine. Date of my parent's wedding anniversary. And my birthday too.' I do not say it aloud, but it is also the date they passed away. So it is a number that is pretty hard for me to forget.

Now there are rumblings from the entire pub and it seems like every pair of eyes are stuck to the screen.

Suddenly, the tension is all too much for me. I cannot take any more. As the balls start to roll out, I break through the crowds and make my way to the cool of the gardens outside.

'You okay?' Hilary calls after me in concern

'Just need some air,' I tell her, 'be back in a second!'

'Deep breaths,' I tell myself. 'Nice deep, soothing breaths.'

And that is when I hear it. A roar starts up inside. Swelling to the levels you would normally only ever hear inside a soccer stadium. People are cheering, whooping and yelling and I don't need to be told what has just happened. It is not hard to guess.

Instead, I just focus on the clear sky above.

'Thank you, Mum,' I find myself murmuring. 'Thank you for my miracle at Midsummer.'

And as if in answer to me, at that exact moment, a familiar looking jeep pulls up right across the road from where a standing.

So he did come then. From where I am standing I can see him clambering down from the car, dark and long and lean. He spots me and strides in my direction.

Andy. Hilary's older brother. Here. And according to Hilary, a newly single man.

'Lizzie!' he beams, as a warm, wide smile crinkles his tanned face. 'Great to see you again!'

'And you!' I manage.

I stutter and try to compose myself. 'Andy, there is something I sort of need to tell you.'

He leans down to peck me lightly on the cheek. Then he cops all the mayhem coming from inside the pub.

'Hey, what the hell is going on in there? Don't tell me that my sister is causing more trouble, as usual?' He grins down at me.

'Ah . . . well, not exactly. That is what I need to tell you. You see . . .'

'Come on inside, Lizzie. Let me buy you a drink and you can tell me all about it.' He drops an arm around my shoulder.

'That would be lovely, thanks,' I tell him playfully. 'But you know, maybe now I can *just* about afford to buy you one.'

A year later

'Ready?' Andy smiles at me.

'You bet,' I beam. I am bursting with happiness as he opens the front door to the Gate House. In the distance I hear the sound of banging and hammering. The builders are working on the big house. It will be beautiful when it is finished. Restored to its former beauty.

Paddy and Jada still cannot believe I did not sell up after my lotto win.

'But you do not need that old ruin. You could buy a big posh pad *anywhere*. The south of France, the Hamptons!' They were so shocked they were babbling.

'I do not want a posh pad somewhere. Radford Hall is my home,' I said firmly. 'And *always* will be,' I added, just so they would not think I was going to change my mind. 'I will be spending *all* my money on it so it won't be a *ruin* for long,' I said coolly. 'Bye.'

I have not seen them since. Mrs Butterly keeps them at bay with the new electric gates and intercom.

'Right, Mrs O'Reilly,' my new husband sweeps me up in his arms. His blue eyes are glinting down at me. Andy is the most handsome man I ever met, and the kindest.

He kicks the door open wider and carries me over the threshold. It is midsummer and the sun streams into our snug new home. Andy bends his head and kisses me. I have never been happier.